Ed's Egg

by David Bedford

Illustrated by Karen Sapp

QED Publishing

Ed loved being an egg.

Ed rolled round and round,
and stood on his shiny
egg head.

Ed blinked in the brightness.
Ed shivered in the coldness.
Ed chirped, "I want my egg!"

Ed did his best to put his
egg back together.

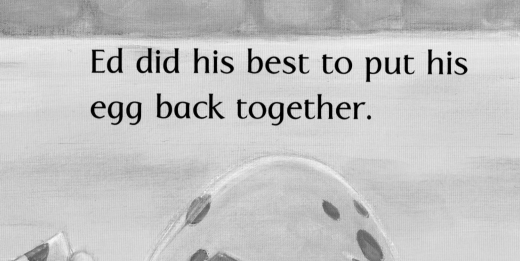

It wasn't too bad, thought Ed.
He could see out, and no one
could see in.

Then Ed heard
a noise...

It was two big ducks, SPLISH-SPLASHING.

Ed could see them, but they couldn't see Ed because Ed was still in his egg.

So Ed joined in the splish-splashing, until...

Three frogs came HOPPITY-HOPPING!

Ed could see them, but they couldn't see Ed because Ed was still in his egg.

So Ed joined in the hoppity-hopping,
until...

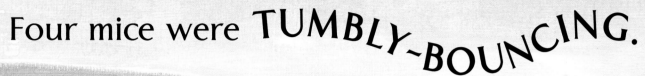

Four mice were TUMBLY-BOUNCING.

Ed could see them, but they couldn't
see Ed because Ed was still in his egg.

Ed joined in the tumbly-bouncing
all by himself.

And he didn't notice something
BIG cluck-cluck-clucking...

Ed tried to hide in his egg, but...
where was it?

Ed shivered. There was
nowhere to hide.

The BIG cluck-cluck-clucker
looked down, and little Ed looked up.
He saw happy eyes and a smiley
beak, and he knew it must be...

"Mum!"

"Hooray!" chirped Ed's brothers and sisters. "Ed is out of his egg."

Ed played SPLISH-SPLASHING,

HOPPITY-HOPPING and

TUMBLY-BOUNCING!

It was fun being out of his egg.

But when he was tired...

Ed wished he still had somewhere cosy
and safe to go.

"We know!" said his brothers
and sisters. "Follow us."
And Ed soon found out that...

"Mums are better than eggs,"
he chirped.

Notes for parents and teachers

- Before you read this book to a child, or children, look at the front cover and ask what they think the story is about.

- Read the story to the children and then ask them to read it to you, helping them with unfamiliar words and praising their efforts.

- Which is the children's favourite picture in the book? Discuss with them why they like it so much.

- Ask the children why they think Ed didn't want to come out of his egg. How do they think he felt inside his egg?

- Discuss with the children what it feels like when they feel shy or scared and want to hide away. Can they think of ways to make themselves feel better?

- Explain to the children how chickens must sit on their eggs to make chicks grow inside them. Sitting on the eggs keeps them warm. Find out how long a mother hen has to sit on her eggs before they hatch.

- Have the children ever seen baby chicks? Do they know what they eat?

- Do the children know any other animals that hatch out of eggs – such as other types of birds, snakes or crocodiles?

- Ask the children to draw a picture of Ed playing with his brothers and sisters. Use paints, crayons or pencils to make it colourful.

Copyright © QED Publishing 2010

This edition published 2013 for Index Books Ltd

First published in the UK in 2010 by QED Publishing
A Quarto Group Company
226 City Road
London EC1V 2TT

www.qed-publishing.co.uk

ISBN 978 1 78171 240 5

Printed in China

A catalogue record for this book is available from the British Library.

Editor: Amanda Askew
Designers: Vida and Luke Kelly